THE DISGUSTING ADVENTURES OF
FLEABAG MONKEYFACE

"WHEN EARWAX ATTACKS"

KNIFE & PACKER

WALKER
BOOKS

The authors would like to dedicate this book to the inventors of the toilet roll, without whom we'd all still be using sticks and leaves – ouch!

First published 2007 by Walker Books Ltd
87 Vauxhall Walk, London SE11 5HJ

2 4 6 8 10 9 7 5 3 1

© 2007 Duncan McCoshan and Jem Packer

The right of Duncan McCoshan and Jem Packer to be identified
as author/illustrator of this work has been asserted by them
in accordance with the Copyright, Designs and Patents Act 1988

This book has been typeset in Shinn Light

Printed and bound in Great Britain by
Creative Print and Design (Wales), Ebbw Vale

British Library Cataloguing in Publication Data:
a catalogue record for this book is available
from the British Library

ISBN 978-1-4063-0305-6

www.walkerbooks.co.uk

A NOTE FROM THE PUBLISHER

We apologize for what you are about to read!

You may want to wear **rubber gloves**. It might also be useful to have a **sick bag** handy; in fact if you've just had a large meal it might not be a good idea to read on at all!

Because this story contains scenes of **extreme grossness**.

So don't tell us we didn't warn you!

But before we get to the gross stuff let's meet our heroes, **Gerald** and **Gene**. They're basically nice kids, but there's a few things you need to know about them:

WANTED

Gene
Likes: Making lists, especially of gross things
Dislikes: Bunny rabbits
Favourite word: "Unreal"
You should know: Gene has the ideas

Gerald
Likes: The sound of a toilet flushing
Dislikes: Clean towels
Favourite word: "Cool"
You should know: Gerald has the stupid habit of liking Gene's ideas

Now let's start at the beginning...

Best friends Gerald and Gene were watching television. The grossest programme on TV, Yucky Science, was about to start. Yucky Science was their favourite programme, and the presenters, Dr Dirk Spamflex and Budgee, the talking budgerigar, were Gerald and Gene's heroes!

In fact Gerald and Gene loved all things gross, and it had got them into some pretty sticky situations!

On a school trip to a farm Gerald was trying to take a closer look at a dung heap when he fell in.

COOL!

UNREAL!

Gene's collection of worms once escaped and took refuge in his bed!

Now these may be situations you would not want to find yourself in, but as we said, Gerald and Gene LOVED all things gross, so they didn't mind at all!

"Pass the popcorn," said Gerald.

"Shhh, it's about to start," said Gene, as the Yucky Science theme tune started.

"Hi gross-out fans and welcome to this week's Yucky Science! Coming up we've got the latest from Slug Safari, later in the programme I'll be taking a close look at a cat's bottom, and Budgee will be buried alive in bogeys. But first a VERY special announcement!"

11

"Thpethal announthment?" said Gene, whose mouth was full of popcorn.

"Thith thounds interethting," said Gerald, as bits of popcorn flew out of his mouth.

"For the first time ever Yucky Science is holding a competition: 'Gloop-Quest'. We want to find the most disgusting gloop ever and we want YOU the viewers to make it. The most stinking, repulsive mixture you concoct will win a very special prize! Tell them what it is, Budgee!"

"The prize for the winner of Gloop-Quest will be an exclusive behind-the-scenes tour of the Yucky Science studio!"

"We've got to enter!" said Gerald, excitedly.

"Never mind enter – we've got to win!" said Gene. "We'll need to come up with something extra-specially disgusting."

2 Meanwhile Gerald and Gene's neighbours and arch-rivals the Smugleys were also sat in front of their TV, watching Yucky Science as they stroked their pet lambs Lamby and Wamby.

Randy and Mandy Smugley were the twins who lived next door. They liked things that were clean and tidy and neat, like their ickle lambs, folded cardigans and puppies. Although they liked nice things, it didn't stop them being nasty – and they had never liked Gerald and Gene.

"This programme is TERRIBLE," said Randy. The only reason they were watching it was because their favourite programme, Fluffily-Wuffily Bunny-Wunny and the Loveable Kittens, was on an hour later than usual that day. "Don't look, Lamby."

"It's making Wamby feel quite queasy," said Mandy. "I bet Gerald and Gene love it."

"I've got an idea," said Randy. "Why don't *we* enter the competition?"

"Now *that* would really annoy Gerald and Gene," chuckled Mandy.

"Imagine their faces if we won!" smirked Randy, as he stroked Lamby.

LET'S GET GLOOPING!

3 "**S**o how are we going to win?" asked Gerald. "There are bound to be other kids who are much better at gross-out science than us!"

"Don't worry, I've had an idea!" said Gene, who, as we've already mentioned, is the one who has the ideas. What we haven't mentioned is that they nearly always lead to something really gross happening.

"Cool!" said Gerald. Gerald, if you remember, is the one who has the stupid habit of liking Gene's ideas.

"Follow me," said Gene. "I'll tell you about it in the Den."

17

The Gross-Out Den was a disused outside toilet at the end of Gerald's back garden, right next door to Gene's.

It was also home to Gerald and Gene's pride and joy: their "Gross-Out Museum". Every shelf was crammed with revolting artefacts they'd collected as souvenirs.

But as they walked to the Den, Gerald and Gene were in for an unpleasant surprise...

The Smugleys were also out in their garden and were busy making their mixture! Not only that but they had the most up-to-date shiny new lab equipment.

"Going to make a gloop in your Den are you?" said Mandy. "I wouldn't bother if I were you! You've got no chance against us!"

"But you hate gross-out," said Gene.

"I know," said Mandy. "So wouldn't it be funny if we won the competition and you lost!"

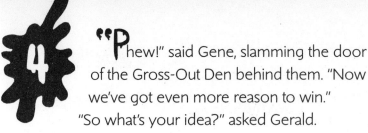

"Phew!" said Gene, slamming the door of the Gross-Out Den behind them. "Now we've got even more reason to win."

"So what's your idea?" asked Gerald.

"Everyone else's gloop is going to be made using stuff you find around the house." said Gene. "We're going to make ours much grosser by adding some 'special' ingredients."

"I like the sound of this," said Gerald. "How 'special?'"

"Very 'special'," said Gene. "We're going to track down the grossest ingredients available to mankind. And forget about high-tech lab equipment like the Smugleys' – we'll use the toilet bowl to make our mix."

"Good idea," said Gerald. "You'll be pleased to hear I haven't washed it ... ever!"

"Unreal!" said Gene. "Now, check out this list of ingredients..."

 That weekend Gerald and Gene used every spare minute they had to track down the ingredients to make their mix. It took them to the most gruesome places.

Firstly they went to visit Jamal Cousins. He'd been off school for a week with a particularly nasty ear infection...

Then they went to Gene's Uncle Germain. He had exceptionally large nostrils, held the local record for sneezing (317 kph) and had had a shocking cold since the 1950s...

And finally they went to Gerald's Aunt Margery. She worked at "The Dog Pound for Strays Suffering From Chronic Runny Bottoms"...

And as each "special" ingredient was added to the toilet, their entry for Gloop-Quest got more and more disgusting...

With their mixture bubbling away nicely Gerald and Gene were having lunch at Gerald's.

"I wonder what Dr Spamflex is doing now?" said Gerald.

"Making TV programmes," said Gene.

"Of course," said Gerald. "That's all he does."

But what they didn't realize was that Dr Dirk Spamflex had a dark secret! Let's join him now, at the Yucky Science Studio...

In a shadowy and dank basement beneath the studio Dr Spamflex was plotting – and what he was plotting had nothing to do with making children's television programmes.

Over the years Dr Spamflex had grown bored of making Yucky Science and only being famous for being on TV. He now wanted more ... much, much more ... in fact he wanted much, much, much more (you get the idea).

"Dr Spamflex, kids' TV presenter, is no longer!" he said from behind a curtain, to his co-host , Budgee. "It's time to meet the new, evil me. Say hello to – **Professor Baaad!!!**"

"What the—?" gasped Budgee.

"And you will no longer be 'Budgee, TV co-host,'" continued Professor Baaad. "You will be a fully-fledged evil sidekick – 'Scary Wings'."

"That's not very – well – scary, is it?" said Budgee. "What about **'Deathbeak, The Bird of Doom'**!!!"

"I love it!" said Professor Baaad. "And look, I've even made you an outfit. Now come with me, Deathbeak!"

Professor Baaad creaked open a large metal door that revealed a huge laboratory, complete with bubbling containers and whirring computers.

"Behold, the **Laboratory of Fear**!" bellowed Professor Baaad, before laughing in a most evil manner – "HAHAHAHAHAHA!!!"

"So what are you filming in here?" asked Deathbeak.

"Filming? Filming? There will be no more filming for me, no more signing kids' autographs, no more being disrespected by the scientific community," replied Professor Baaad. "Because I'm going to be too busy TAKING OVER THE WORLD!!!!" And with that he laughed a particularly loud and unpleasant laugh – "HAHAHAHAHAHA!"

7 Meanwhile Gerald and Gene finished their lunch, unaware of their hero's evil plans.

"Don't throw away those chicken bones, Mum," said Gene. "Those will go great in the mixture."

"There you go," said Gerald's mum, putting them in a bag. "And I've also thrown in some rotten bananas I found in the back of a cupboard."

"These bones and mouldy bananas should be the final ingredients," said Gene as they walked to the Den. Fortunately there was no sign of the Smugleys.

"I can't believe anyone's gloop is going to be more disgusting than ours," said Gerald. "Not even the Smugleys'. Let's just hope Dr Spamflex is impressed."

KEEP STIRRING, GERALD!

MORE CHICKEN BONES, GENE!

Gerald and Gene spent the whole afternoon putting the final touches to their experiment...

Early the next morning a huge gale started to brew. There was thunder and lightning, and rain came pouring down. In fact the storm was so loud that it woke both Gerald and Gene.

"Cool!" shouted Gerald to Gene. As we've already mentioned Gerald and Gene were next-door neighbours, and their rooms were really close to each other.

"Unreal!" shouted Gene.

But their excitement soon turned to horror as they witnessed something extraordinary happen ... suddenly there was a huge bolt of lightning!

"Oh, no – the Den!" cried Gerald.

"It's taken a direct hit!" replied Gene.

As if the Den being hit by lightning wasn't incredible enough, neither of them could have predicted what was about to happen next...

The whole building began to shake and shudder ... it was glowing and vibrating as it briefly left the ground. But what Gerald and Gene couldn't see was what was causing this: the gloop in the Den toilet was gurgling and fizzing.

As the shelves wobbled objects started to fall into the toilet: a dictionary, the jar of fleas, the false teeth, in fact the whole Gross-Out Museum!

Finally there was a huge...

9 **G**erald and Gene grabbed the first clothes they could get hold of and ran down to the Den. From inside they could hear strange gurgling noises.

As Gene carefully opened the door they couldn't believe their eyes.

"The place is wrecked!" said Gene.

"And what is that smell?" asked Gerald nervously, sniffing the air.

"I don't know, but I think it came from over there," said Gene, pointing at the toilet, which was bubbling and gurgling alarmingly.

OUR GLOOP!

"It must have reacted with the lightning," said Gerald. "We wanted to create the most disgusting substance in the world ever – and it looks like we've done it!"

The gloop certainly looked and smelled foul and it was now behaving very strangely indeed...

"It's moving," said Gene nervously.

Now, as lovers of all things gross, Gerald and Gene had seen some pretty disgusting things – but nothing could have prepared them for what was going to happen next.

The pile of gloop started to rumble ... then it began to wobble ... and then it started making strange noises.

"I can handle our disgusting gloop," said Gerald. "But what's going on now?"

Then, with a gigantic squelching noise, a small hairy hand emerged...

An arm appeared ...

then an elbow ...

48

then a shoulder ...

then:

It was the most disgusting thing they'd ever seen in their lives. A hairy head smeared in cheese appeared. It was burping and dribbling and the banana breath was like nothing they'd ever smelt before...

Now, we could go into a lot of scientific mumbo-jumbo, but you wouldn't find that very interesting. To cut a long story short the lightning had caused a reaction in the toilet bowl, fusing the ingredients. In the intense heat, the contents of the Gross-Out Museum, the DNA in the old cotton buds and hankies, the old banana and all the other revolting things had combined.

Without meaning to, Gerald and Gene had just created something strange, disgusting and **ALIVE!**

10 **"W**hat a fleabag!" said Gene, waving away the flies. "Unreal!"

"Have you ever seen a monkey face like that before?" said Gerald, holding his nose. "Cool! But how did that happen?"

"By exploding earwax, banana and bogey, I suppose. Not to mention the entire contents of the Gross-Out Museum." said Gene. "Looks like we've accidentally made a strange monkey-creature. Yikes!"

UG–HELLO

said the creature.

"It talks!" said Gerald. "How is that possible?"

"Well, there was a dictionary in the Museum," said Gene. "It must have absorbed the entire contents!"

"It also explains why he's covered in fleas," said Gerald. "I told you we shouldn't keep live fleas in there. But why does he have smelly cheese on his face?"

"I was ug-hungry. I ug-ate your lunch..." interrupted the creature.

"Lunch? That must be the packed lunch from the Gross-Out Museum! It's been there for two years!" said Gene. "And you ate it?"

"*Gross out!*" said Gerald and Gene together.

"Ug-delicious," said the creature. "Although the egg wasn't ug-rotten enough for my ug-liking."

"Wow!" said Gerald. "What's your name?"

"I don't have an ug-name," said the creature, picking a flea from his bum and eating it. He was clearly still hungry. "Any ug-ideas?"

Gerald and Gene tried all kinds of names, but none of them sounded right.

Then Gene realized they had the name all along:

"I've got an idea. Why don't we call him **Fleabag**?" said Gene. "**Fleabag Monkeyface**!"

"Brilliant!" said Gerald.

"Fleabag Monkeyface... I ug-love it," said the creature, farting loudly. "So this is my ug-room?"

"Er, well, I suppose so." said Gerald. "What are we going to do with him?" he whispered to Gene.

"We made him ... I think we should keep him." Gene whispered back.

And so Gerald and Gene decided to adopt Fleabag Monkeyface.

LOOKS LIKE HE'S HERE TO STAY!

11 But as Gerald and
Gene were adopting a new
friend, things were getting even more
sinister back at the Laboratory of Fear.

"Soon, Deathbeak, we will take over the world!!!"
said Professor Baaad.

"And how exactly do you plan to do that?" asked
Deathbeak.

"With a monster," said Professor Baaad
triumphantly.

"A monster?" said Deathbeak nervously. "But where are you going to get this monster from?"

"Aha," said Professor Baaad. "By using yucky science of course. Whilst you've been asleep at night, I've been working in this lab. Hour upon hour, night upon night – trying to create a monster."

"I thought you were building a new set for Slug Safari," said Deathbeak.

"Foolish bird," said Professor Baaad. "I have invented a machine that can turn any gloop into a monster! Behold, the **Monstermatic™**!"

"Monstermatic?" said Deathbeak.

"The nastier the gloop, the bigger the monster," said Professor Baaad. "And using a gloop of my own making, made up of various disgusting ingredients, including my own earwax, the **Monstermatic™** has made a monster."

"**Are you ready to confront the beast?**" said Professor Baaad, in an unnecessarily booming voice.

ARE YOU READY FOR **FEAR?**

"Er, yes?" said Deathbeak...

ARE YOU READY FOR **TERR-OR?**

continued Professor Baaad. "Er, I suppose so," muttered Deathbeak.

ARE YOU READY FOR **HORR-OR?**

"I'm not too sure," whimpered Deathbeak. "Then meet the monster!" – and with that Professor Baaad *opened up his hand...*

59

"It's minute!" said Deathbeak, trying not to sound too disappointed.

"But vicious," said Professor Baaad. "I just need to make him bigger. To do that I need a stronger, more disgusting gloop."

"Where are you going to get that from?" asked Deathbeak.

"Gloop-Quest, of course," said Professor Baaad. "I'm sure one of our viewers will provide the gloop that we need ... HAHAHAHAHAHAHAHA!"

TAP TAP TAP

12 Back at the Gross-Out Den Gerald and Gene had more pressing concerns than Professor Baaad and the **Monstermatic™**. Because just then there was a loud tap at the window...

"Oh no it's the Smugleys," said Gene. "Quick – hide Fleabag."

"What do you want?" asked Gerald, stashing Fleabag behind the toilet.

"We heard the commotion and just had to come and have a look," said Randy and Mandy. "So what exactly is going on? Lamby and Wamby are quite distressed."

61

Before Gerald and Gene could say "Private Property", the Smugleys were in the Den, poking around. It didn't take long for them to find Fleabag. "And what have we here?" said Randy.

"A monkey-creature – yuck!" said Mandy. "Hey, that's cheating. You can't use zoo creatures to help make your mixture."

"And you can't keep him here," said Randy. "Look at all those fleas. He's probably contagious! Come here Lamby and Wamby, get away from the nasty creature." And with that he grabbed Fleabag Monkeyface.

"You can't do that," said Gerald, but the Smugleys, were heading back to their house. "Put him down!"

"We're going to do everyone entering Gloop-Quest a favour and take him back to the zoo," said Mandy.

"I've got a better idea. We could take him to the vet's," said Randy. "The vet will probably put him down!"

Fortunately though, Fleabag had a surprise up his hairy sleeve; something even *he* didn't know about – until then. Slowly but surely Fleabag started to get irritated...

"The monkey creature is starting to look a bit cross," said Randy, looking down at Fleabag, who was starting to growl. Lamby and Wamby had already rushed for cover.

"And why are his nostrils flaring?" asked Mandy.

"What's going on?" whispered Gerald.

"No idea," replied Gene. "But he looks pretty mean!"

It didn't take long to find out...

As everyone was about
to discover, an angry Fleabag had
some potent weapons – and right now
he was pretty angry. In fact he was so
angry that he took careful aim and with a loud
grunt fired a volley of **supersonic bogeys** at the
Smugleys!

"Euuuaayuck!" screeched Randy and Mandy, as
they were splattered in green slime. "Get it away from
us! You won't get away with this! We're still going to
win!!!"

Gerald and Gene quickly scooped up Fleabag as
the Smugleys fled.

"That was unbelievable," said Gerald.

"So he's got Gross-Out Power!" said Gene, as Fleabag got back to his usual self.

"Go to the ug-vets, no ug-chance," said Fleabag. "I'm staying ug-right here!"

"Of course you are," said Gerald. "We'll just have to make sure it's OK with my parents!"

13 But before they could present him to Gerald's parents they had to perform a monkey-makeover:

First they sat him in a hot bath for a looooooooooong time (and he was still a bit smelly!)

They combed his hair – this was a two man job!

They then found some of Gerald's old clothes that fitted him...

Finally they set up his new home. They made him a bed in the old toilet in the Gross-Out Den, gave him his own key and made him promise not to eat any future exhibits in their Gross-Out Museum.

Finally, a scrubbed-up, suited-and-booted Fleabag Monkeyface was ready to meet the parents!

Before entering the kitchen Gerald and Gene gave Fleabag Monkeyface a final briefing:

"Remember the house rules: no picking your nose," said Gerald. "No eating nits ... and NO Gross-Out Power!"

"And try to keep your banana breath under control," said Gene. "We'll wait here. Gerald will go in first to explain..."

14 Fortunately Gerald's parents were the understanding sort. They had to be, because with Gerald for a son disgusting things were always happening in their house, not to mention the old toilet at the end of the garden.

"Mum, Dad," said Gerald nervously. "Remember you told me I wasn't allowed any more pets?"

"Yes," said Gerald's dad. "That was after your pot-bellied pig ate my trousers and we had to take him back to the pet shop."

"Well what would you say if I told you I've got a new – er – pet," continued Gerald. "But this time I promise to look after him?"

"Pet?" said Gerald's mum suspiciously.

"Well he's not exactly a pet," said Gerald. And with that he opened the door to let in Fleabag.

UG-PLEASED TO MEET YOU

Fleabag was on best behaviour and trying to look as cute as possible.

"Pleased to meet you," said Gerald's mum. "Of course he can stay!"

(Well, that's Gerald and Gene's version of what happened. In reality when the parents met Fleabag, Gerald and Gene had to do so much begging, grovelling, and promising to clean out toilets that it's too nauseating even for this book! As much to shut up Gerald and Gene as anything else, Fleabag was finally allowed to stay...)

A delighted Gerald and Gene left the kitchen. In the hall Fleabag had put on one of Gerald's mum's hats and was wiping his nose on Gerald's dad's best coat.

WIPE
SNUFFLE

And so Fleabag Monkeyface settled in to his new home.

"It's so cool having you live here," said Gerald.

"I'm ug-delighted," said Fleabag.

"You've got school tomorrow," shouted Gerald's mum. "And don't forget your swimming trunks!"

"I'd almost forgotten." said Gerald. "It's the school swimming gala."

"Taking Fleabag in should be interesting," said Gene. "I wonder if he can swim?"

15 The next day, Gerald, Gene and Fleabag Monkeyface set off for school. They just hoped their new friend wouldn't cause too much of a stir.

"With any luck no one will notice that he's just a little bit different," said Gerald, who had lent Fleabag one of his old school uniforms.

"He's just a bit hairier than the other kids," said Gene hopefully. As they walked down the street towards school Fleabag was scratching his bum and eating a flower. "And his behaviour is a *bit* stranger..."

When they got to school the hairy new kid was the last thing on the minds of the children there. With the annual school swimming gala happening that day, everyone was too excited to notice.

Mr Troutman, their teacher, added the new kid's name to the register.

"Fleabag Monkeyface? That's an unusual name," said Mr Troutman. "Can you swim?"

"I ug-think so," said Fleabag, whose only experience of swimming was in a toilet bowl full of gloop.

It was only when they reached the swimming pool that Fleabag began to make his presence felt.

"This soup is ug-delicious!" said Fleabag, wiping his lips.

"That's not soup – that's the anti-verruca foot-pool," said Gene.

GROSS OUT!

GROSS OUT!

"**GROSS OUT!**" shouted the other kids.

"Quiet in there," said Mr Troutman, who had changed into his gym kit. "First race, 50 metre freestyle. I want Josh, Samantha, Ramesh, Mary, Nate, Gerald, Gene and ... what was it again? Oh yes, Fleabag."

"Typical," said Gerald. "We've been put up against the best swimmers. We've got no chance."

SWIMMING GALA

As Gerald predicted, after the first length the three of them were lagging seriously behind.

"He did ug-say freestyle, didn't he?" asked Fleabag.
"Er – yes," said Gene nervously. "Why?"
"I thought I would ug-give us a little ug-boost," said Fleabag. "Time for an ug-**turbo fart**!!!" Before Gerald or Gene could stop him Fleabag's face scrunched up in concentration...

There was a loud gurgling noise, the water started to foam – and suddenly the three of them were being swept past Ramesh, Josh and the rest!

"This is amaaaaaaaazing!" shouted Gerald. "You've created a mini tidal wave!"

"We've won!" shouted Gene as they reached the end of the race – in joint first position!

"Gerald, Gene and Fleabag!" shouted a fuming Mr Troutman. "Out of the pool now. You're disqualified!"

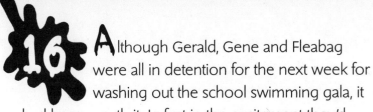

Although Gerald, Gene and Fleabag were all in detention for the next week for washing out the school swimming gala, it had been worth it. In fact in the excitement they'd almost forgotten why they'd accidentally made Fleabag in the first place...

"Hey! It's the Gloop-Quest competition tomorrow," remembered Gene suddenly.

"And our gloop turned into Fleabag," said Gerald. "We'll never win that tour of the studio."

"Where are we going to find something gross to show Dr Spamflex?" said Gene scratching his head.

"How about ug-this?" said Fleabag removing a finger from his ear. At the end of it was a great big blob of the most repellent-looking earwax.

The next day, full of confidence, the three of them set off to the Yucky Science studio, clasping a jar containing a large globule of Fleabag's earwax . Surely no one could have made a gloop more gross than theirs.

Their mood soon changed when they arrived. A huge queue of kids stretched around the block, all clasping pots and buckets containing their disgusting looking gloops. Worse still, right in front of them were the Smugleys!

"Well, if it isn't Gerald and Gene," said Mandy. "And they've brought their little friend – how sweet!"

"I don't know why you've bothered to turn up," said Randy. "You'll never beat our gloop. In fact, it's so strong we're having to wear these protective suits."

81

"You haven't seen what's in our jar!" said Gene, holding up the bubbling jar of earwax.

"Earwax! Is that the best you could do?" said Mandy.

"Our gloop contains a two-year-old rotten egg, three bags of vacuum cleaner fluff and a litre of concentrated cat pee!" said Randy.

But before Gerald or Gene could reply they realized they were getting close to the front of the queue...

17 And there was Dr Spamflex himself! At least it looked like Dr Spamflex, but he was nothing like he was on TV. Instead of being cheerful and funny he was distinctly grouchy, and as each kid arrived before him, he took one look at their gloop, then dismissed them!

"I'm a very busy man so let's just get on with it," groaned Dr Spamflex, as he peered into yet another bucket of gloop.

"He's never this grumpy on TV," whispered Gene.

In fact Dr Spamflex and Budgee seemed completely bored by the whole process. And as each contestant showed them their gloop, they got the same treatment.

"Mmm, mixing old tea bags and soup, pathetic," yawned Dr Spamflex. "Goodbye!"

"An apple core placed in a fizzy drink, you call that gross!?!" barked Dr Spamflex. "Go away!"

Then it was the turn of the Smugleys...

"Egg, fluff and cat pee – hmm," mused Dr Spamflex. The Smugleys grinned at Gerald and Gene. "Nice suits, but your gloop is rubbish."

"But Dr Spamflex—" wailed Randy and Mandy.

"That's it, I've had enough. I give up!" said Dr Spamflex. "Come on Budgee, we'll just have to make our own gloop. The competition is off!"

Randy and Mandy looked like they were about to burst into tears. But Gerald and Gene had no time to talk to them as they rushed past to catch up with Dr Spamflex.

"Dr Spamflex! Dr Spamflex!" shouted Gerald. "Have a look at our gloop, *please*?"

They caught up with him just as the studio door was about to shut.

"Oh very well," said Dr Spamflex in his grumpiest voice yet – but, holding up the bubbling jar they'd brought in, he seemed genuinely interested for the first time.

"Now this is more like it," said Dr Spamflex. "So what have we here?"

IT'S FROM MY UG-EARS!

"It's chemically enhanced earwax," said Gene, trying to make it sound as scientific as possible.

"It's from my ug-ears," said Fleabag, proudly. "But Gerald and ug-Gene should take the credit."

"Now *this* stuff is interesting," said Dr Spamflex, fixing his eyes on Fleabag Monkeyface. "The winners of Gloop-Quest are Gerald, Gene and their ... furry ... thing. Step inside the studio ... oh, and do bring your little friend along!"

18 Gerald and Gene didn't even have time to wave to the Smugleys as the Yucky Science studio doors shut behind them. In fact they didn't even have time to congratulate each other before Dr Spamflex started the tour. They found themselves being swept through the studio, and in each room there was something new and disgusting – but Dr Spamflex seemed to be in a big hurry.

"And now to the final room of the tour," said Dr Spamflex, opening a small side door.

"But we wanted to see more of the maggots," said Gerald, who was sure he'd just seen Dr Spamflex wink at Budgee.

"Yes, and I wanted to see where you film Slug Safari," said Gene.

"There's no time for that," said Dr Spamflex gruffly. "I'm a busy man, I've got a World to take—"

"—gross-out films to," interrupted Budgee, before Dr Spamflex could give the game away.

"Exactly! So, gentlemen, follow me," said Dr Spamflex, "and behold: the oldest camel poo in the world!"

As they entered the room Gene immediately
noticed that Dr Spamflex and Budgee had put on
gas masks.

"Shouldn't we get one of those?" asked Gene.
There was the most sickly smell
coming from the poo.

But before Dr Spamflex
could reply Gerald, Gene
and Fleabag were
beginning to feel drowsy.
"I think I'm going to fall
asleeeeeeeeeeeeeep,"
said Gerald.

19 With Gerald, Gene and Fleabag snoozing on the floor, Dr Spamflex explained his dastardly plan to Budgee.

"This jar of earwax isn't nearly enough," said Dr Spamflex. "We need to get the monkey creature to the Laboratory of Fear, extract the mother lode of earwax, and return him here, unharmed, as soon as possible."

"His earwax?" asked Budgee.

"Yes! When the **Monstermatic™** gets hold of that stuff it will make a monster ready to take over the world in no time!" said Dr Spamflex.

After placing Fleabag on a trolley, they made their way to the Laboratory of Fear as quickly and as quietly as they could. They only just had time to stop off and change into their evil outfits.

"Ah, that's better," said Professor Baaad as they reached the door of the Laboratory. "I feel so much more nasty in my evil-suit."

Once in the laboratory, Fleabag was strapped onto an operating table.

"Let the earwax extraction commence!" said Professor Baaad, and then laughed his most evil laugh yet...

Professor Baaad stood behind a control desk as a huge laser device was lowered from the ceiling, pointing straight at Fleabag.

"Commence earwax extraction!" boomed Professor Baaad, pressing a button on the control panel. The laser shuddered into action and then fired at Fleabag. With a loud gurgling noise the machine began to remove the yellow gunge that Professor Baaad wanted so desperately.

"It's working!" cried the evil TV presenter. "It's working – AHAHAHAHAHAHAHAHAHAAA!"

"That's more than enough," said Professor Baaad, admiring the large vat of yellow gloop. "My monster will be ENORMOUS!"

"Hadn't we better get the creature back to his friends?" said Budgee, who had hidden behind a computer throughout the procedure.

"Of course. And off with the outfits – there will be plenty of time to wear them later, when we're taking over the World!"

"**W**ake up, wake up!
You must have passed out from the fumes." came a
voice.

"What happened?" asked Gerald, rubbing his eyes.

"You were overpowered by the stench of that
camel poo," replied Dr Spamflex. "I should have
given you gas masks, but I forgot."

"How long did we pass out for?" asked Gene.

"Oh, only a couple of minutes," fibbed Dr Spamflex.

"My ug-ears feel strange," said Fleabag, rubbing his
head.

"Well, that's the end of the tour," said Dr Spamflex, as he hurried Gerald, Gene and Fleabag to the exit. "It was great having you here."

"We, er, really enjoyed it," said Gene, who was still feeling a bit drowsy.

"Until the camel poo room, anyway," added Gerald. "Thanks for having us."

"No, thank *you*," said Dr Spamflex, fixing Fleabag with a stare and letting off a muffled evil laugh. "In fact I really can't thank you enough!"

"Don't we get to ask you some questions?" asked Gene hopefully.

"I've not got time for that," said Dr Spamflex in a grumpy voice. "I've got to go to the laboratory to do some, er, um, filming."

As Gerald, Gene and Fleabag walked home, they were still puzzled by Dr Spamflex's behaviour.

"He wasn't as nice as he is on TV," said Gene. "It was like he couldn't wait to get rid of us."

"I never thought we'd leave feeling queasy," added Gerald. "What was that camel poo room all about?"

"And my ug-ears still don't feel right," said Fleabag.

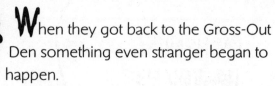

21 When they got back to the Gross-Out Den something even stranger began to happen.

"I'm hearing ug-voices," said Fleabag.

"Voices?" said Gene.

"Yes, voices in the ug-house," said Fleabag. "Your ug-dad's on the ug-toilet and just asked your ug-Mum to bring up some more ug-toilet roll because he's run out"

"But you can't hear people talking in the house from here," said Gerald.
"That's impossible!"

105

"Well I ug-can," insisted Fleabag. "And not only that but I can also ug-hear a centipede ug-farting on a cabbage leaf three gardens away."

FFRPT!

"A centipede farting? But that's ridiculous. Your hearing is usually quite bad," said Gerald – who didn't want to be rude and say that it was because of the amount of earwax in Fleabag's ears.

"Maybe we should have a closer look at your ears," suggested Gene. "Something is obviously not right..."

Gerald produced a large magnifying glass and the two of them peered into Fleabag's Monkeyface's ear. What they saw was shocking.

Fleabag's ear was sparkly and minty fresh. Not just that, there was no unpleasant smell and no weird creepy crawlies!

"Unbelievable!" said Gerald.

"Unreal!" said Gene. "It's almost like it's been completely cleaned out. No wonder your hearing has gone supersonic. This is strange, very strange."

22 But of course if Gerald and Gene had known what had happened at the Yucky Science studio they would have realized there was nothing strange about it at all. In fact it was hardly surprising that Fleabag's ears were so clean – their entire supply of earwax was now in a large bucket in Professor Baaad's Laboratory of Fear. And Professor Baaad just could not wait to get the Monstermatic™ to work on it.

As soon as Gerald, Gene and Fleabag had left the studio, Dr Spamflex ran to his laboratory as fast as his little legs could carry him. No sooner had he whipped on his evil outfit than he set to work on the precious earwax.

He examined it under a mammoth microscope.

He mixed it with every chemical he could lay his hands on.

And finally he blasted it with lasers and electricity.

Until, finally, after working round the clock for several days, the mixture began to bubble and boil and was ready for the **Monstermatic™**.

Professor Baaad called Deathbeak into the laboratory.

"Deathbeak, I've done it!" cried out a jubilant Professor Baaad – and there, behind a curtain, was the outline of a huge monster.

"I've done it! By using that monkey creature's earwax the **Monstermatic™** turbo-boosted my previous, feeble effort. Behold, **The Ear Thing**!" – and with that he let out an *almighty* evil laugh. "AHAHAHAHAHAHAHAHAHAHAHAHA!!! Soon the whole world will shudder at the very mention of the name!"

AHAHAHAHAHAHA

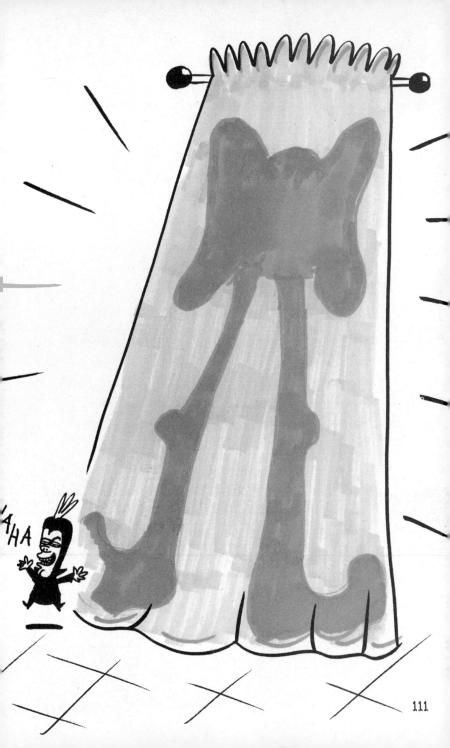

"It certainly looks impressive," said Deathbeak, taking a peek behind the curtain. "But is that the best name you could come up with, 'The Ear Thing'?"

"Well, that's what it is," said a deflated Professor Baaad.

"I know," said Deathbeak. "It's just that if you're going to take over the world with it, don't you think the name should sound a bit, well, meaner?"

"Yes, yes! Good idea," said Professor Baaad. "What about The Aural Ogre!"

"Too scientific," said Deathbeak.

"OK, OK then... What about the Wax Organism?" said Professor Baaad. "Don't tell me that doesn't sound scary."

"Give me strength," sighed Deathbeak. "Too long-winded. I've got it! What about **EARMAGEDDON**?"

"Earmageddon! I love it!" shouted Professor Baaad. "All we need now is the perfect time to unleash him – and I know just the occasion!"

RUB RUB

"The Yucky Science Roadshow!" said Gerald excitedly, looking up from the newspaper. "It's next week!"

Every year Yucky Science held a Roadshow, and this year it was at the local mall. There were stalls and talks and a chance to get up close and personal with the latest stuff they were filming. There was no way Gerald, Gene and Fleabag were going to miss out on this.

"Can't wait," said Gene. "Do you remember what happened last year?"

The year before, everything had been running smoothly at the Yucky Science Roadshow – until Gerald and Gene showed up. They were working on a school project about Creepy Crawlies along with their friend Andy Splash. Andy was already wishing he hadn't agreed to help Gerald and Gene...

"OK Andy," said Gerald, "we need a close look at these cockroaches. Let's get closer to the enclosure," said Gerald.

"But I'm scared of cockroaches," said Andy. "I'd rather not."

"C'mon Andy," said Gene. "Look: they're all feasting on a bit of rotten fish. This is great!"

"Oh, all right," agreed Andy finally. "But I'm not going too close."

But as the three of them pressed up against the cockroach enclosure there was a deafening *crack*! The side of the enclosure had broken and Andy had fallen in!

"Get them off me, get them off me!" screamed Andy. "One of them has got down my shirt!"

"Gross-out break dancing, cool!" said Gerald.

"That was brilliant!" said Gene. "So, what's happening at this year's Roadshow?"

"Dr Spamflex himself is giving a speech!" said Gerald. "He will unveil something 'No Gross-Out Fan Will Want To Miss'. Cool!"

"Unreal!" said Gene.

"Ug-brilliant!" said Fleabag.

24 But Dr Dirk Spamflex was not writing a speech. In the Laboratory of Fear, top to toe in his Professor Baaad suit, he was preparing for World Domination!

"Soon my friend, soon. The day approaches!" cackled Professor Baaad. "And the world will be mine!!! AHAHAHAHAHAHAHA!!!"

"Aren't we supposed to be taking over the world *today*?" asked Deathbeak.

"Oh – yes, it is today!" cried Professor Baaad. "AHAHAHAHAHA!!! To the Baaadmobile!"

Outside the Yucky Science studio, at a secret exit, Professor Baaad had parked the Baaadmobile...

"I can't wait to see their faces at the mall," laughed Professor Baaad, "when they get a load of Earmageddon and his instantly-sticking wax. As soon as it touches any living thing it sets rock hard – just ask the Laboratory of Fear gerbils!"

"Now, are you sure you packed everything we need?" asked Deathbeak. "Evil monster to take over the world?"

"Check!" said Professor Baaad.

"Spare Evil Suit in case one gets dirty?" asked Deathbeak.

"Check!" said Professor Baaad.

"Cheesy bread?" asked Deathbeak.

"Cheesy bread? Why would I need cheesy bread?" said Professor Baaad. "This is World Domination I'm planning, not a picnic!"

"You know how grouchy you get when you miss a meal," said Deathbeak. "Don't worry if you haven't packed lunch. You can always have some of mine. I've got plenty of spicy sunflower seed..."

"I'll grab some cheesy bread on the way," said Professor Baaad. "Now to the mall!"

"Via the International Cheesy Bread Bakery!" said Deathbeak. And with an extra loud evil laugh they were on their way!

The World of **SMELLY HATS**

Slightly Grubby Socks Slideshow

A Vaguely Unpleasant ANT

25

As Professor Baaad and the Baaadmobile
sped towards the mall, Gerald, Gene and Fleabag
were just arriving.

"This has to be the worst Roadshow ever," said
Gene. "Just look at these stalls and attractions: *'Slightly
Grubby Socks Slideshow'*; *'The World of Smelly Hats'*;
'A Vaguely Unpleasant Ant'."

"It's pathetic," said Gerald. "It's like they haven't even
bothered this year."

"And I was so ug-excited," said Fleabag.

"If it wasn't for Dr Spamflex's speech I'd just go
home," said Gene. "He did promise us something
'No Gross-Out Fan Will Want To Miss'."

"It had better be good," said Gerald. "But where is Dr Spamflex? His speech should start any minute."

No sooner had Gerald finished his sentence than all the lights in the mall were dimmed and loud rock music started to blare out.

On stage the Yucky Science Cheerleaders started to sing: "Gimme a 'Y'! Gimme a 'U'! Gimme a 'C, K, Y'! Whaddya got?"

"YUCKY!" shouted the crowd.

"Looks like the speech is about to start," cried Gerald.

"Quick, let's get front row seats," said Gene, as the three of them rushed towards the stage.

"But where ug-is he?" asked Fleabag, as they tried to catch sight of Dr Spamflex.

Then they spotted him.
TV's top gross-out presenter
was being lowered from
the roof of the mall.

"It's certainly ug-spectacular,"
said Fleabag, as the whole crowd erupted
with applause and cheers.

Dr Spamflex landed on the stage just as the applause reached a climax.

"Greetings all, greetings all," beamed Dr Spamflex, who seemed to have a strange glint in his eye. "It's great so many of you came along. And I'm sure you'll all *stick around!*" With that he let out a muffled evil laugh. "Now if you thought I was here to tell you about dandruff, droppings or dirt—"

"Yes, ug-tell us about ug-dandruff, droppings and dirt!" shouted Fleabag, but Dr Spamflex just glared back at him.

"I'm sorry to disappoint you! Because this year I'm planning something much, much more spectacular!!!" He stepped into a small cubicle. "Budgee, hit the lights!"

There was a series of explosions and fireworks, followed by darkness. The whole crowd oohed in anticipation...

Then with a blinding flash of light a spotlight picked out a figure on the stage. Dr Spamflex was almost unrecognizable!!!

"What's going on?" asked Gerald.

"And why is Dr Spamflex wearing a ridiculous outfit?" added Gene.

"Hush and tish to you all! Dr Spamflex is no more. Say hello ... to **Professor Baaad**!" The crowd gasped. "And this is no longer my co-host Budgee," continued Professor Baaad. "This is my evil sidekick –
Deathbeak, The Bird Of Doom!"

"What's going on?" said Gerald.

"I don't know," said Gene. "But it might explain some of his weird behaviour!"

"I think we're about to ug-find out," said Fleabag.

26 "**N**ow you've met the new me, you'll want to hear my speech," said Professor Baaad in a mocking voice – before whispering to Deathbeak, "This is all going quite well isn't it?"

"Just get on with unveiling the monster."

"My speech is entitled: '**How To Take Over The World Starting With The Mall**'!" – and with that Professor Baaad let out a shop-shuddering laugh.

Now, at this point you might expect the whole place to panic with people fleeing the mall, but everyone was too stunned to move.

"I've had enough of being treated like a second-rate celebrity!" boomed Professor Baaad. "I want more! Much, much more! It's time to say hello to my little friend!!!"

He pulled a lever and the curtain behind him was swept up and away – to reveal ...

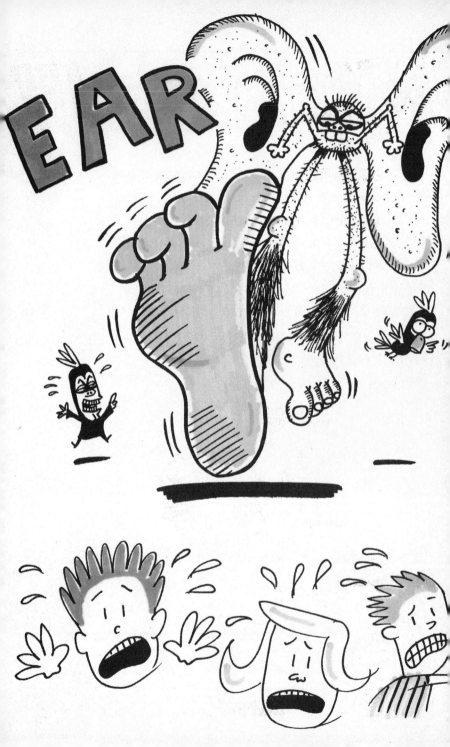

MAGEDDON!!!

"EARMAGEDDON!!!" cried Professor Baaad.

Now there *was* panic in the crowd. People shouted and screamed and fled. Everyone, that is, except Gerald, Gene and Fleabag. Something this gross was too good to miss!

"Cool gross-out monster!" said Gerald.

And things were about to get a whole heap grosser – as Earmageddon was about to reveal his secret gross-out weapon!

27

"Not so fast!" came a shrill voice from the back of the crowd.

"Oh no," said Gerald. "It's the Smugleys!"

"You'll never get away with this," said Randy. "We've been training our pet lambs!"

"Lamby, Wamby, attack!" shouted Mandy. But as soon as the two lambs made for the stage Professor Baaad's voice boomed out: "Earmageddon! **Unleash your weapon!!!**"

Upon Professor Baaad's command Earmageddon sprang into life. At first it shook its head... Then it took aim with its ears. The crowd gasped...

"Now fire!" shouted Professor Baaad. The earwax monster started to fire volleys of a yellow gloop at Lamby, Wamby and the Smugleys.

"What is that stuff?"
said Gene as they ducked behind their seats. "The Smugleys have been frozen like statues."

Earmageddon was now unleashing his wax on the crowd – all around them, people were getting stuck by the vile sticky missiles.

"It seems to be some sort of super-strength earwax," said Gerald, looking at a dollop of the yellow goo.

"It looks familiar," said Gene.

"You can ug-say that again," said Fleabag, sniffing the mixture.

"Fleabag! Of course!" said Gene. "But where did Professor Baaad get it?"

"Fools!" said the Professor, who had overheard their conversation. "Although I should thank you – your hairy friend was most kind to donate his wax at the studio. The **Monstermatic™** couldn't have done it without him!"

"So that's what happened when we passed out," said Gene. "Dr Spamflex, or should I say Professor Baaad, must have taken Fleabag away and extracted some of his earwax!"

"Then mutated it into this monster," said Gerald. "We've got to stop him!"

SNIFF
SNIFF

Earmageddon, meanwhile, was running riot in the mall. Shop by shop, restaurant by restaurant, the whole place was grinding to a halt under a blanket of earwax.

"As soon as we have waxed the mall we will wax the world!" crowed Professor Baaad. "Next stop the International Cheesy Bread Shop – I'll never have to pay for cheesy bread again!"

"I think we should strike something a bit more impressive than the International Cheesy Bread Shop," said Deathbeak.

"Oh, like the trouser factory! Or where they tin pineapples," said Professor Baaad.

"No! Like the most important building in town," said Deathbeak.

"Trumpet Tower!"

Trumpet Tower was the pride and joy of local billionaire Donaldus Trumpet, owner of the TV station that broadcast Yucky Science.

"Yes! Yes! Trumpet Tower, of course," cried Professor Baaad. "I'll show him who's boss! To the Baaadmobile!"

Professor Baaad, Deathbeak and Earmageddon left the devastated mall – and Gerald, Gene and Fleabag needed a plan, quick.

"If Earmageddon is made out of Fleabag's wax, then the only way to stop him is to fight wax with wax," said Gene.

"Do you think your Gross-Out Powers can handle it?" Gerald asked Fleabag.

"I'll give it an ug-try," said Fleabag, whose ears had refilled with wax since the trip to the Yucky Science studio.

"Cool!" said Gene. "We need to follow Professor Baaad and Deathbeak and get out of the mall. I've got an idea!"

28

Outside the mall Earmageddon carried on his rampage. He strode through the streets towards the city centre, waxing all before him, as Professor Baaad and Deathbeak followed in the Baaadmobile.

"This is beyond my wildest dreams!!!" cackled Professor Baaad, who was getting very excited and jumping about in his seat. "Nothing can stop Earmageddon!!!"

"Perhaps I'd better drive," suggested Deathbeak.

"Indeed, Bird of

Doom, take the wheel while I throw back my head and commence some really evil laughter as my beautifully evil plan comes together – er, beautifully! HOOHAHAHAHAHAHA!!!"

But what they didn't realize was that the Baaadmobile was carrying some extra passengers...

"Great plan, Gene," said Gerald. "They won't be able to shake us off now."

"We need to corner Earmageddon and hope that Fleabag's Gross-Out powers can defeat him," said Gene.

Just then the Baaadmobile screeched to a halt.

"Trumpet Tower," said Gene. "I should have guessed. So this is where Professor Baaad plans to take over next."

"We can't let him get away with it," said Gerald. "Are you ready, Fleabag?"

"Just give me the ug-signal," replied Fleabag.

But before Fleabag could unleash his powers, Professor Baaad had spotted them in his rear-view mirror.

"Looks like we've got company," cackled Professor Baaad. "Great to have you along. Sit back and enjoy while I take over the world! AHAHAHAHAHAHA!"

"No," said Gene, trying to sound as calm as possible. "We're going to stop you taking over the world!"

"Now even I find *that* funny," said Deathbeak, as the two of them erupted with hysterical laughter. When Professor Baaad finally stopped laughing, he wiped a tear from his eye and said, in a very nasty voice, "I suggest you go home.

"Unless you
want to join me in the
Laboratory of Fear – where this time I
will extract earwax from all three of you!"
Just then the foot of Trumpet Tower began to
shudder and shake …

Earmageddon was at the very top of Trumpet Tower, showering all around him in earwax. Police helicopters and planes were buzzing him, but he just swatted them away.

"We have to go up if we're going to have any chance of defeating him," said Gerald.

"I've got an idea," said Gene. "The lift!"

142

Fortunately Professor Baaad and Deathbeak were too busy laughing maniacally to notice the trio sneaking into Trumpet Tower.

"Top floor," said Gene, as they entered the lift. In no time they whizzed to the top of the building.

"This door looks like it leads to the roof," said Gerald.

"Let's get ug-ready to ug-rumble!" said Fleabag, as they pushed it open.

Suddenly they were very close to Earmageddon, who was busy spraying the city below in noxious earwax – until he noticed that he had company.

"He's coming towards us!" said Gerald. "I think he's taking aim!"

Earmageddon had
temporarily stopped his
destruction of the city and now
seemed determined to get rid
of the three new arrivals.

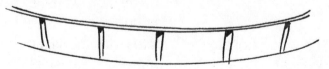

"OK Fleabag, over to you!"
gulped Gerald.

"Time for Gross-Out Powers!"
said Gene.

Fleabag didn't need to be asked
twice, and he started to growl...

GRRRRRRR

ROAR !!!

The Gross-Out Powered Fleabag let off a mighty roar, but Earmageddon seemed completely unworried.

"Quick, Fleabag!" said Gene. "We're about to get glooped!"

Fleabag was soon at eye level with Earmageddon –

and just in time he unleashed a full volley of supersonic bogeys.

"Phew!" said Gerald. "That was close!"

"He's giving him both barrels! Go Fleabag!" shouted Gene. "Soften him up with bogeys!"

At first the monster seemed confused. But the volley of bogeys was just bouncing off him!

147

"It's not working!" cried Gerald.

"Try the earwax!" shouted Gerald.

"Ug-good idea," said Fleabag. He pointed an ear at the Ear Monster and let rip with a round of earwax pellets.

Now the monster was really angry – he'd definitely had enough of Fleabag.

Earmageddon was now firing with all his might straight at Gerald, Gene and Fleabag. But Fleabag's wax was stronger ...

...and he was blasting Earmageddon's sticky wax straight back at him!

"It's working!" said Gerald.

"Pin him down," said Gene.

Using every ounce of earwax he had, Fleabag finally blasted Earmageddon against a wall.

"He's trapped in his own
earwax!" cried Gerald.
"You've done it!" shouted Gene. Earmageddon
was now completely out of action!

"Well done Fleabag – your Gross-Out Powers have saved the World!" said Gerald.

"Let's get back to ground level and make sure Professor Baaad and Deathbeak haven't escaped," said Gene.

"I can't wait to see their faces," said Gerald. "They won't be laughing now!"

30 Back at the foot of Trumpet Tower, Professor Baaad was waiting for them – but he was still laughing!

"So your furry friend got lucky and defeated Earmageddon," said Professor Baaad.

"Yes, your bid to take over the world is over," said Gene, proudly.

"Do you really think so?" said Professor Baaad. "I've got one more surprise up my sleeve – AHAHAHAHAHAHA!"

There was a roar in the distance, and a strange and sinister vehicle appeared...

At the wheel was Deathbeak.

"Prepare for doom!" roared Professor Baaad. "When I had your monkey thing in the lab I also removed a bogey and some phlegm – and in an operation so top secret not even I knew what I was doing, the **Monstermatic™** manufactured two other monsters!"

"Two more monsters!" said Gene.

"Make that three," said Professor Baaad. "I also made a backup Earmageddon: the all new and improved **Earmageddon II**, now with hairy ears. It's time to meet the **Ear, Nose and Throat Monsters**! AHAHAHAHAHAHAHHA!!!"

Deathbeak opened the back of the vehicle he'd driven up in.

"This way my beauties," said Deathbeak. "It's time to get busy!"

Three huge creatures lumbered out of the lorry, and awaited Professor Baaad's command to take over the world one bit at a time...

One by one Professor Baaad gave the order to his beasts.

"**Nostrildamus**, it's time to blow!" commanded Professor Baaad.

The nose monster started to spray a green bogey-like liquid.

"**Coughzilla**, unleash your great balls of phlegm!!" commanded Professor Baaad.

The throat creature began coughing nasty great globules at the buildings.

"**Earmageddon II**, wax at will!" commanded Professor Baaad.

Now Earmageddon II joined in the chaos, raining down earwax.

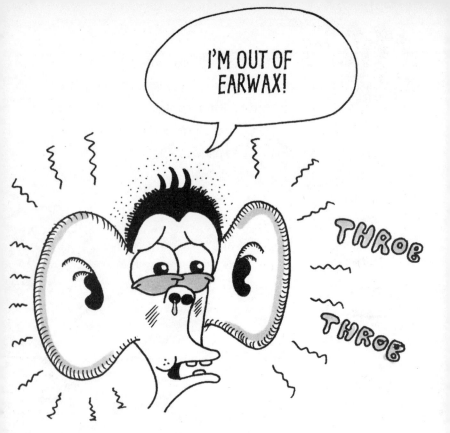

With three monsters running riot it was once again time for some Gross-Out Power ... but Fleabag was out of earwax!

"I ug-used it all on Earmageddon," said Fleabag. "It'll take ug-days for me to have enough to ug-defeat them."

Fortunately Gene had been thinking. "I've got an idea," he said.

31 "It had better be extra good," said Gerald, as the monsters run amok around them.

"It is good – in fact it's super-extra-good with sprinkles," said Gene, trying to sound as confident as possible. "I've made a list."

"List?" said Gerald, who didn't really think it was the time for lists.

"Yes, a list of what we'll need to defeat the monsters. Fleabag, I need you to fetch the giant flagpole from the top of Trumpet Tower. Gerald, you need to go to Uncle Germain's and get the biggest hanky he's got. I'm going to the mall to get Lamby and Wamby."

"But!" said Gerald.

"No buts," said Gene. "I'll explain when we've got the stuff!"

So off they set, ducking and diving to avoid the carnage around them.

"See how they flee!" laughed Professor Baaad. Fleabag scaled Trumpet Tower as quickly as his hairy little legs could carry him, whilst Gerald dashed off to Uncle Germain's and Gene set off to grab Lamby and Wamby.

32 It didn't take long for the three of them to return with their items.

"Our only chance of defeating a giant ear, nose and throat is to think big!" said Gene. "And with Fleabag out of earwax, we'll need to use some of your other Gross-Out Powers."

"Yes, but what about this stuff?" asked Gerald.

"Uncle Germain's hanky will stifle the Nose Monster," said Gene. "Use a mega-sneeze to get above Nostrildamus, then drop it. That should smother him!"

"Ug-good idea," said Fleabag, grabbing the flag – Nostrildamus was right behind them!

Grabbing the huge hanky,
Fleabag mega-sneezed above
the monster, then, on Gene's
command, dropped it.
Confused by the giant hanky the
Nose Beast started to run around
in circles.

"It's out of control!"
screamed Gerald. "What
are we going to do?"
But before Gene could
answer, Nostrildamus ran
into a building – it
was out cold!

THUD!

"Bless you!"
shouted Gene.
"Now to
Earmageddon II!"

163

It didn't take long to find, and with its hairy ears it was unleashing even more mayhem than Earmageddon. As the creature loomed over them Gerald still didn't know how they were going to take it on.

"Nice hanky-work on Nostrildamus," said Gerald. "But how are we going to defeat this?"

"By thinking big," said Gene. He stuck Lamby and Wamby at either end of the flagpole Fleabag had got from the top of the tower. "Behold the largest cotton bud – ever!"

"OK, Fleabag," said Gene, handing Fleabag the oversize cotton bud. "Distract Earmageddon II with some banana-breath, then stick it to him!"

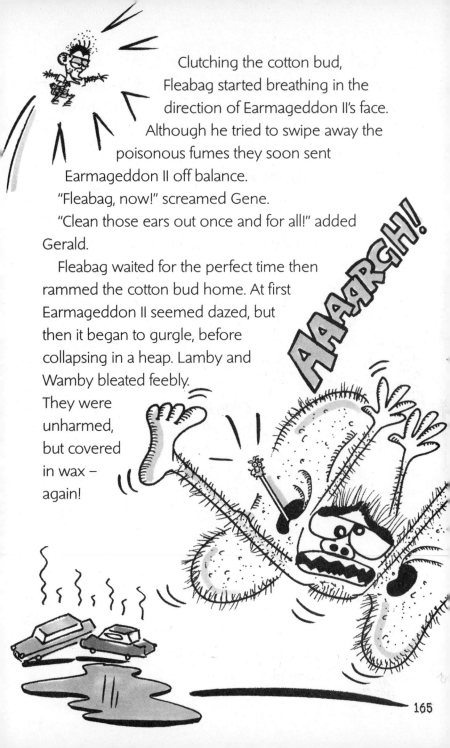

Clutching the cotton bud, Fleabag started breathing in the direction of Earmageddon II's face. Although he tried to swipe away the poisonous fumes they soon sent Earmageddon II off balance.

"Fleabag, now!" screamed Gene.

"Clean those ears out once and for all!" added Gerald.

Fleabag waited for the perfect time then rammed the cotton bud home. At first Earmageddon II seemed dazed, but then it began to gurgle, before collapsing in a heap. Lamby and Wamby bleated feebly. They were unharmed, but covered in wax – again!

AAAARGH!!

With two
of his monsters
out of action Professor
Baaad, Deathbeak and
Coughzilla rushed to the scene.
"My monsters – what are you doing
to them?" screeched Professor Baaad,
standing in front of his last remaining beast. "Well, you
will never defeat Coughzilla! AHAHAHAHAHAHA! The
world will still be mine!!!"

"So what's the plan?" whispered Gerald, urgently.

"The only way to defeat a Throat Monster is by getting
something stuck in it," said Gene. "Something BIG!"

"Yes, but what?" asked Gerald.

"Professor Baaad and Deathbeak, of course!" said
Gene. "Fleabag, time for the biggest turbo-fart ever!"

Fleabag bent over and carefully took aim.

"What's he doing?" screeched Professor Baaad.

"I don't like the look of this," wailed Deathbeak.

Even Coughzilla was taking notice!

"Now fire!" shouted Gene.

The surrounding buildings shuddered as Fleabag let rip. With a huge squelching noise Professor Baaad and Deathbeak were blasted into Coughzilla's throat"

"**GROSS OUT!**" shouted Gerald and Gene. Even Fleabag looked impressed at what he had just done.

SSSSSQUELCH!!!

"How dare you!" yowled Professor Baaad. "Coughzilla, spit us out!"

But Coughzilla had his mouth full and began to splutter – then crumpled to the ground, with Professor Baaad and Deathbeak still trapped in his jaws.

"You wait 'til I get out of here," said Professor Baaad. "Deathbeak, do something!" But Deathbeak was stuck fast!

"Ug-losers!" chuckled Fleabag.

"Face it, Dr Spamflex, it's game over," said Gene.

"Don't call me that, I'm Professor Baaad," wailed the former TV star.

"To think we used to really like you and your show..." said Gerald.

By the time the police arrived Fleabag Monkeyface was back to his usual (slightly hairy) self.

"Congratulations, kids – looks like you saved the world from hideous monsters," said the Police Commissioner, shaking all of their hands. He looked suspiciously at Fleabag. "How did you do it?"

"Oh, with a bit of gross-out power," chuckled Gene.

"Well, there's someone who'd like to meet you," said the Commissioner. It was local billionaire and owner of the Trumpet Network, Donaldus Trumpet.

"You saved the world, not to mention my Tower," said Donaldus Trumpet. "How can I ever thank you? You can have anything you want!"

33 With Dr Spamflex and Budgee now retired (well, in prison, actually) Donaldus Trumpet was only too happy to agree to what Gerald and Gene asked for: their very own TV programme!

With Gerald and Gene behind the camera and Fleabag as their new presenter, "Yucky Science" became "Gross-Out TV" ...

...but to discover what they filmed you'll have to read the next 'Disgusting Adventure of Fleabag Monkeyface' – which makes this one look like an episode of "Fluffily Wuffily Bunny-Wunny and the Lovable Kittens" – don't say we didn't warn you!!!

If you can't wait until the next
Fleabag Monkeyface book, here's
a free comic to keep you going.
(It makes perfect on-the-toilet reading!)

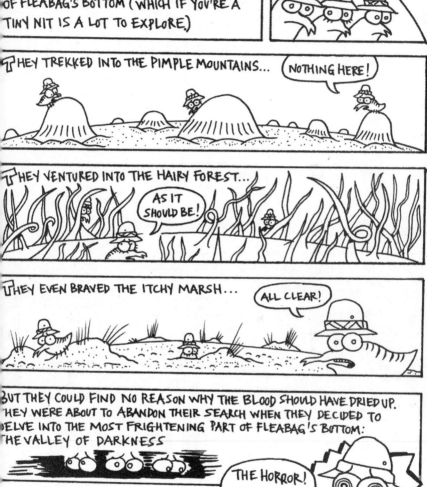